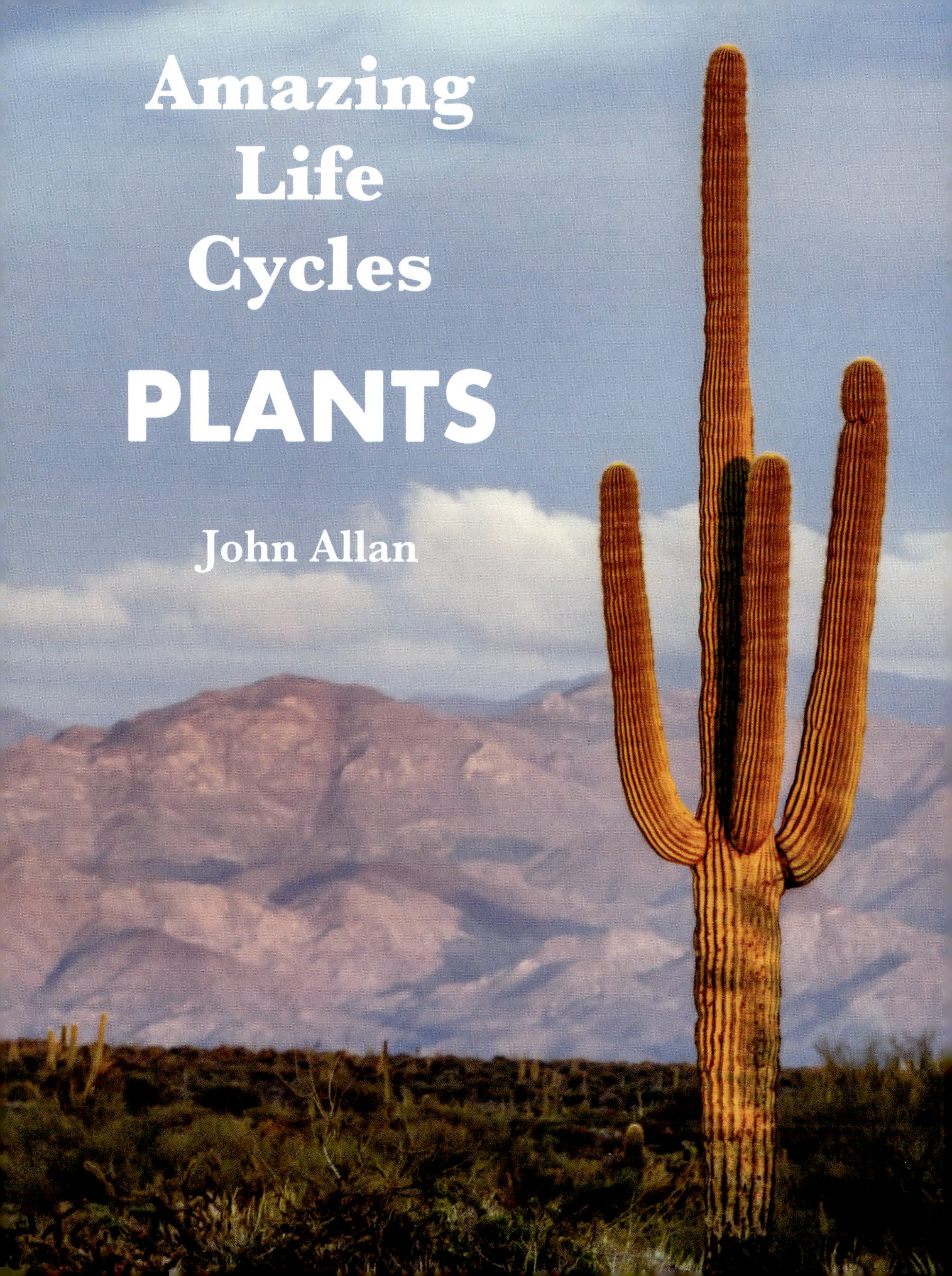

Amazing Life Cycles

PLANTS

John Allan

A maroon-eyed tree frog takes a rest on an insect eating Red Pitcher plant

Contents

What is a plant? 4

Parts of a plant 6

Plant habitats 8

Seeds and bulbs 10

Scattering seeds 12

What is a life cycle? 14

Amazing plant life cycle: Rafflesia 16

Amazing plant life cycle: Pitcher plant 18

Amazing plant life cycle: Saguaro cactus 20

Amazing plant life cycle: Coconut palm 22

Amazing plant life cycle: Squirting cucumber 24

Amazing plant life cycle: Baobab tree 26

Amazing plant life cycle: Resurrection fern 28

That's amazing! 30

Glossary and index 32

Words that look **bold like this** are in the glossary.

ISBN 978-1-912108 053

First published in Great Britain in 2019 by
Hungry Tomato Ltd, The Old Bakery Studios, Blewetts Wharf,
Malpas Road, Truro, Cornwall, TR1 1QH, UK

Manufactured in the United States of America

We eat the fruits of an orange tree.

What is a plant?

Plants are living things which grow out of the ground. Most plants produce flowers,* fruits, *and* seeds. *Plants come in many different shapes and sizes. Trees and shrubs are also plants.

Grass is a plant which is eaten by many animals.

Some flowers have a sweet smell which attracts insects.

Most plants make flowers which are usually brightly colored.

Flowers attract birds and insects. The birds and insects help the plant to **reproduce**.

AMAZING PLANT FACT

A tree is a plant. Some trees can live for hundreds or even thousands of years.

Mosses and ferns are plants which do not produce flowers. They grow in places where there is not much light.

Wheat is a type of plant with seeds that we call grain. We cannot eat the grain raw, but we can make it into flour and use it to make bread.

Parts of a plant

This bird of paradise plant has a flower that looks like a bird!

Plants have a root, stem, and leaves. Most plants have roots which grow in the ground. The roots push down into the soil to hold the plant in place. Above the ground is the stem, leaves, and flowers.

Plants can make their own food inside themselves. The plant's leaves use sunlight to make food for the plant.

The plant's stem carries food from the roots to the other parts of the plant. It also carries the leaves towards sunlight.

The plant's roots suck up water and **nutrients** from the soil to feed the plant.

The parts of a plant can come in many different shapes, sizes and colors.

The plants above are living stone plants. They have two thick leaves which look like stones, or pebbles, on the ground.

The stems of some plants grow around other plants. Lianas (right), which grow in **rainforests**, do this.

A tree has a hard woody stem called a trunk.

Plant habitats

This saguaro cactus grows in deserts.

A habitat is the place where a plant or an animal lives. Plants can grow in many different habitats including under the sea!

Plants live in most of the world's habitats.

Habitats map

Map key

This map key shows you what the colours and pictures on the map mean.

- Temperate grasslands – areas that are dry in summer
- Tropical grasslands – hot, dry areas with few trees
- Tundra – cold, windy places
- Cool, rainy forests
- Arctic/Antarctica – frozen, snowy ground and icy seas
- Cold forests
- Warm, wet rainforest
- Deserts – dry land with little rain

AMAZING PLANT FACT

The greatest number of different plants grow in warm, wet rainforests.

The sharp prickles on a cactus are actually the plant's leaves. The prickles lose less water than normal leaves in the hot **desert** habitat.

On the cold, icy Arctic tundra plants, grow in clumps low to the ground to avoid the wind.

AMAZING PLANT FACT

Some Arctic plants have hairs on their leaves, stems, and buds to protect them.

In the ocean, long strands of seaweed grow under the sea. Seaweed is a plant without roots. It has a special part called a holdfast to keep it in one place.

Seaweed uses the holdfast to cling to rocks.

The black dots in this kiwi fruit are the seeds.

Seeds and bulbs

New plants can grow from a seed or a bulb. A seed is like a small case which contains everything needed to make a new plant.

AMAZING PLANT FACT

Insects, such as bees and butterflies, visit flowers to drink sweet **nectar**.

In winter, the plant above the ground dies. When the weather becomes warmer, new leaves grow out of the bulb.

A bulb grows at the bottom of the plant under the ground. During the summer, the plant stores food in the bulb.

This wasp is covered in pollen from the anthers of a flower.

Insects, such as bees, carry pollen from the anthers of one flower to the stigma of another flower. This is called **pollination**. After pollination a seed is made.

Most plants have flowers. The flower's anthers are covered in a fine yellow dust called **pollen**.

In the middle of the flower are the stamens, the male parts. Each stamen has an anther at the top. The female part is called the carpel. It has a section called a stigma at the top.

Each dandelion seed blows to a new place to live.

Scattering seeds

Plants have many ways of making sure their seeds find a way of leaving the mother plant and growing in a new place. Some plants are blown away from their mother plant by the wind.

AMAZING PLANT FACT

Birds eat seeds in fruit. The seeds pass through the birds and fall to the ground in their droppings. The seeds grow into new plants.

This macaw is eating a green chilli.

Some animals help spread seeds. Squirrels eat acorns. They collect them and bury them.

Inside the acorns are the seeds of the oak tree.

Tumbleweed is a bush which breaks away from its roots in the autumn. The wind pushes it along the ground, and it scatters its seeds as it rolls along.

What is a life cycle?

Sunflower seeds are a tasty snack for birds and people.

A seed lands in the soil. A root grows down from the seed into the soil.

The seeds fall to the ground. Birds eat the seeds and spread them in their droppings.

Plant Life Cycle

The plant makes new seeds.

Insects pollinate the flower.

A life cycle is all the different* stages *and changes that a plant or animal goes through in its life. This diagram shows a plant life cycle.

A shoot starts to grow above the ground from the seed. The shoot in this picture is covered by the seed's outer coat.

Tiny leaves appear on the shoot.

The shoot grows taller and stronger. More leaves grow. The leaves get bigger.

A bud appears and grows into a flower.

Rafflesia

AMAZING PLANT LIFE CYCLE

This is the bud of a rafflesia flower.

Before a plant can make a seed, it has to be pollinated. This is done by insects that land on the plant and carry the pollen to another plant.

AMAZING PLANT FACT
The rafflesia is the world's biggest flower! It grows to nearly 3 feet (1 m) across the middle.

Many plants have colorful flowers and a strong smell that attracts insects. The rafflesia has a terrible smell.

The flower appears when the plant is ready to be pollinated. It smells of rotten meat or rotten eggs. Flies love this smell and are attracted to the flower.

The rafflesia grows in rainforest habitats in Southeast Asia.
The rafflesia has no leaves, just a giant flower that lives for only a few days.

AMAZING PLANT LIFE CYCLE

Pitcher plant

Pitcher plants come in lots of different shapes and colors.

Pitcher plants grow in rainforests and places where the ground is damp. Pitcher plants are **carnivorous** ***plants—this means they eat meat. They have a special bowl, or pitcher, which traps small insects.***

AMAZING PLANT FACT

Some pitcher plants eat snails, frogs, and even small mice!

A jumping spider is hiding from the rain in a pitcher plant. Or will it become a tasty meal?

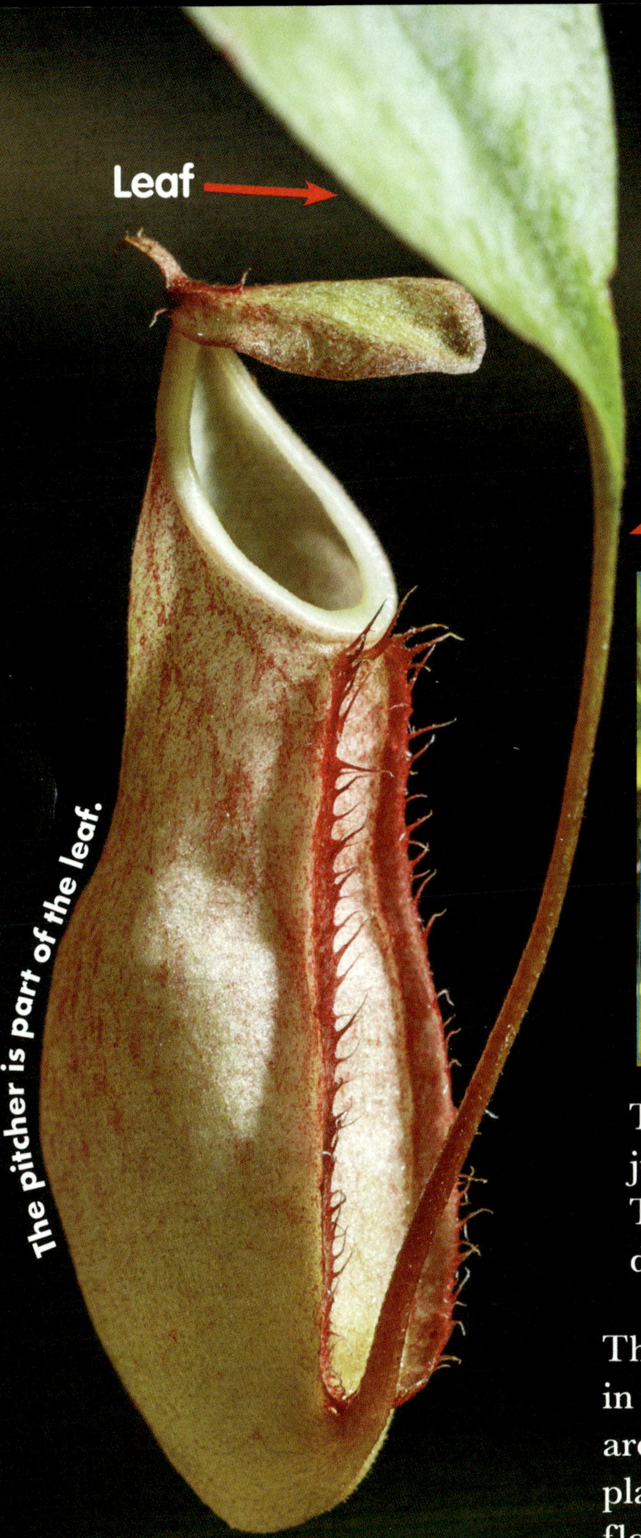

The pitcher is like a thin tube. When insects come to taste the sweet juice inside the tube, they slide down the slippery sides and cannot get out again.

The insects drown in the pool of juice at the bottom of the tube. Their body is broken down and digested by the plant.

The pitcher plant grows flowers in early spring. These flowers are pollinated by bees. The plant makes seeds inside the flowers. The seeds fall to the ground when they are **ripe**.

The pitcher is attached to the leaf by a long, thin tendril.

AMAZING PLANT LIFE CYCLE

Saguaro cactus

Gila woodpeckers make nest holes in the saguaro's trunk.

The saguaro cactus plant can live for 100 years. When the saguaro is about 35 years old, it begins to produce flowers.

AMAZING PLANT FACT

Saguaro flowers open in the middle of the night and close up at lunchtime the next day.

Bats, bees, and birds feed on nectar from the flowers. They pick up pollen from the flowers on their bodies.

The saguaro cactus stores water in its trunk.

Buds appear in spring on the top of the main trunk and arms. The buds open into large, white flowers.

When the animals carry pollen from one cactus to another, pollination happens and the cactus produces seeds.

This Gila woodpecker carries pollen from cactus to cactus.

The plant's prickles stop animals from eating it!

AMAZING PLANT LIFE CYCLE

Coconut palm

The white part inside a coconut is called meat, which we can eat.

Coconut palm trees have male and female flowers growing on the same tree. When the tree has flowered, it makes new seeds. The fruits of a palm tree are called coconuts.

Coconut palms often grow on beaches. Many coconuts are washed out to sea. They float along until they land on another beach.

Young coconuts are filled with sweet liquid.

When the coconut reaches a new place, shoots will start to grow. This new palm tree will be ready to flower and produce seeds in about seven years.

AMAZING PLANT FACT

Coconut shells can be used to make pots and cups.

Coconuts grow in bunches under the palm tree's leaves.

When the coconuts are ripe, they fall to the ground.

Inside the skin of a coconut is a thick, hairy covering. Under the covering is the seed coat which has three "eyes." The new shoots grow from the eyes.

Squirting cucumber

The plant's yellow flowers are pollinated by insects, such as bees.

The squirting cucumber grows on sandy or stony ground. The plant has a thick, hairy stem which trails along the ground. The fruit of the plant is long and green. It looks a bit like a small, hairy cucumber.

Seed

There are about 25 to 50 seeds in each fruit.

Fruit

AMAZING PLANT FACT

The seeds of the squirting cucumber shoot out of the fruit at up to 62 mph (100 km/h)!

The fruit fills up with juice and seeds. It gets fatter and fatter. When the fruit is ripe, it suddenly explodes! The seeds inside are fired out like bullets.

Gourd plants have fruits with a hard outer covering.

The squirting cucumber belongs to a group of plants called gourds. The fruits can be dried, and the empty shells can be used to make cups, bowls, or musical instruments.

Baobab tree

Baobab trees live on hot, dry grasslands in Africa. When it rains, the tree can store up to 26,500 gallons (100,000 L) of water in its trunk—enough to fill a garden-sized swimming pool!

These are the seeds from inside the baobab fruit.

You can see the flower's anthers.

The tree stays bare for nine months of the year. Then it grows leaves and flowers. The big, white flowers open up during the night.

The flowers smell sweet and attract night time animals, such as bats. The animals get pollen on their bodies and help pollinate the flowers. Then the tree produces big fruit.

Animals that eat baobab seeds spread them in their droppings.

Baobab seeds are eaten by elephants, antelopes, and monkeys.

The baobab is also called the upside down tree because it looks as if its roots are growing at the top of the tree.

AMAZING PLANT FACT

A baobab tree starts flowering when it is about 20 years old. It can live for up to 3,000 years!

Resurrection fern

A fern's leaves are called fronds.

This fern lives by attaching itself to another plant. It lives on large trees, such as oak trees. The fern gets the water and nutrients it needs from the **bark** ***of the tree and from the air.***

The fronds of the resurrection fern turn brown, shrivel up, and look dead when there is no rain. The fern can live like this for years.

AMAZING PLANT FACT

Resurrection means "to come back to life." This fern got its name because it almost dies and then comes back to life again!

Ferns do not make seeds. Instead, they have tiny spores that are so small you need a microscope to see them.

When a spore lands on a new place to live, it grows a very thin root called a rhizoid. This root supplies the spore with water. The spore grows into a new fern.

These brown spots are called sori. The spores are inside the sori.

After just one rain shower, the fronds uncurl, turn green, and seem to come back to life.

That's amazing!

Do you like eating these seeds?

Plants are a very important part of every habitat. Plants give animals and people food and shelter. In return, animals can help plants survive in lots of ways!

Some plants have flowers that look like insects or birds, like this bee orchid. This tricks insects and birds into visiting the plant.

This is the Methusela tree, which is 4,850 years old and the second oldest tree in the world.

The venus fly trap is another meat-eating plant. Here it has captured an insect. It will take over a week to fully eat it's prey.

AMAZING PLANT FACT

This is the dragon blood tree. It oozes red resin from it's bark, which gives it its unusual name.

A burr is a seed with a prickly covering.

Sometimes animals brush past plants that have burrs. The burrs get stuck in the animals' hair or fur and are carried to a new place where the seed can grow.

Glossary

bark – the outer layer of a tree's trunk
carnivorous – the word to describe an animal or plant that eats meat
compost – dead leaves and bits of plants that have mixed together and become crumbly and full of goodness
desert – a very dry place that is often sandy or rocky. Deserts can be very hot in the day. Some deserts get cold at night.
fruits – fleshy parts grown by a plant that contain the plant's seeds
nectar – a sweet liquid inside flowers. Insects and birds drink nectar
nutrients – substances found in food that nourish animals and plants
pollen – a special dust produced by plants. Pollen is needed to make seeds.
pollination – when pollen is carried from the anthers of one flower to the stigma of another flower
rainforests – forests of tall trees in places with lots of rain
reproduce – to make seeds that will grow into new plants. To have babies.
ripe – ready to grow
seeds – small parts of a plant. Seeds leave their parent plant and find a place where they can grow into a new plant.
soil – the layer of earth in which plants grow
stages – different times of a plant's life when the plant changes in some way

Index

A
acorns 13
animals and plants 4, 11, 12, 13, 14, 17, 18, 21, 26, 30, 31
B
baobab trees 26, 27
bee orchids 30
bird of paradise plants 6
buds 10, 15, 16, 21
bulbs 10, 11
burdock plants 31
C
cactus 8, 20, 21
carnivorous plants 18, 19
coconut palm trees 22, 23
D
dandelions 12
dragon blood tree 31
F
ferns 5, 28, 29
flowers 4, 10, 11, 14, 16, 17, 19, 20, 21, 26, 31
fruits 4, 10, 13, 24, 25, 26
G
gourds 25
grain 5
H
habitats 8, 9
L
lianas 7
life cycle diagram 14, 15
living stone plants 7
M
mosses 5
O
oak trees 13
orange trees 4
orchids 31
P
palm fruit 22
pitcher plants 18, 19
plants 4, 5, 6, 7
pollination 11, 14, 17, 19, 21, 26, 31
R
rafflesia 16, 17
resurrection ferns 28, 29
S
saguaro cactus 8, 20, 21
seaweed 9
seeds 4, 10, 11, 12, 13, 14, 15, 19, 21, 22, 23, 24, 25, 26, 31
shrubs 4
smell 4, 16, 26
spores 29, 30
squirting cucumbers 24, 25
T
trees 4, 5, 7, 13, 15, 22, 23, 26, 27
tumbleweed 12

Picture credits

Shutterstock. 1: Ray Redstone. 4-5: VAlekStudio, Pirasoot, serkan mutan, Dewin, Indew, Nitr, chittakorn59. 6-7: symbiot, asharkyu, Akugasahagy, Chansom Pantip, Rasulov. 8-9: Aura Bliss, Scisetti Alfio, Bildagentur Zoonar GmbH, divedog. 10-11: Roman Samokhin, RTimages, suzz, Lilkar. 12-13: enstantoni MDSABBIR, Aimee Lee, Maciej Bledowski. 14-15: Mykhailo pavlenko, wk1003mike, Bo1982, ZaZA studio, Pearl-photogrpahy, Daniel G, ER-09, taviphoeo, BigBlueStudio, Ian2010. 16-17: Stephanie Bidouze, Herrieynaha, Somsak. 18-19: Jefff Holcombe, Eric Krouse, Linas T. 20-21: Charles T Peden, Tom Roche, tntphototravis. 22-23: Tim UR, Nonnakrit, Ozerov Alexander, Ethan Daniels, Iakovleva Marina. 24-25: ozgur kerem bulur, ANGHIi, SaskiaAcht, Sandy Morelli. 26-27: Dennis van de Water, ninette_luz, Francisco Hererera, Dave Montreuil. 28-29: tome213, Nichole Casebolt, Sam Aronov. 30-31: Yoyochow23, Rudmer Zwerver, Heather Lucia Snow, Kuttelvaserov Stuchelova, Anna_Polyakova.